D0122200

J E D

Sixteen-year-old Jed was thinking that Mississippi was a mighty long way from Wisconsin. Jed was a Yankee soldier. He had been through the Battle of Shiloh. Now he was stationed in Mississippi, where the countryside had been swept clean by the Union raids.

Jed was a tested Army man, a veteran fighter — but today he was just a homesick boy. He missed the green Wisconsin hills, the smile of his mother and the friendship of Will.

Then Jed found the young southern boy with a broken leg. Against the boy's protests, Jed had the leg set and took the boy back to his home deep in the Mississippi hills.

For a few hours Jed found the warmth and friendship of a home among people who were supposed to be his enemies.

Written with simple honesty and warmth, JED is the moving story of the soldier who was not yet a man.

JED
THE STORY OF A YANKEE SOLDIER AND A SOUTHERN BOY

BY PETER BURCHARD

Drawings by the author

Coward-McCann, Inc.   New York

Fifth Printing

Library of Congress Catalog Number: 60-12479

Manufactured in the United States of America

TO BETSY

AUTHOR'S NOTE

This is the story of a 16 year old Yankee soldier and a Mississippi boy in the fall of 1862.

My thanks go to Guy and Elinor Deming for their help with the manuscript, to J. Walter Strong of Elkhorn, Wisconsin and Claude F. Eames the present editor and publisher of the THE ELKHORN INDEPENDENT for their letters about the history of Elkhorn and other parts of Walworth County.

During the Civil War THE INDEPENDENT was published by a man named Frank Leland. Little is known of Leland except that the paper improved under his leadership. The paper supported Lincoln and when he was shot the column rules were turned upside down making heavy black borders for mourning.

CHAPTER ONE

SOMETIMES Jed knew it was good he had Will Smith's teaching to remember. Will had told Jed why the War had started and what the North was fighting for. Jed had taken Will's love of Abe Lincoln to himself. When Will told one of Lincoln's funny stories he spoke with a special softness in his voice.

Will knew a lot about Abe before most folks around Elkhorn had ever even heard of him. He had told Jed that Lincoln worked hard as a boy, that he understood people and that he'd even done a little soldiering.

Now Jed was far from Wisconsin and Will Smith. He was in the state of Mississippi. Since the battle near Shiloh Church, all the glitter and promise had gone out of soldiering. He had fought in a peach orchard, and he remembered the blossoms falling like snow as they were hit by a hail of bullets. He had taken memories from Shiloh that would stay with him the rest of his life.

Now Jed leaned against the wheel of a wagon with his boots in the mud. His trousers were dirty, and there was a big three-cornered tear in the right leg. He had patched it together, but it still let in the cold. He wore a Federal blue uniform jacket buttoned right up to the neck. Jed was lean and hard, and the jacket looked big on him. A rag of a red kerchief stuck out above his collar, and his cap was tilted back so his red-brown hair fell over his forehead.

Jed knew he had to be alone and this place was as much alone as he could get. He hoisted himself up onto the wagon and sat there looking out across the lowland to a little rise where the sun was dipping red behind the streaking clouds, making the sky look as if a great brush had swept once across it. Now he found himself stirred by gentler, more distant memories.

He could scarcely remember his ma, though he did have two or three faded pictures of her in his mind. He remembered walking with her to the Walworth County Fair and holding tight to the pink tickets that he'd been given for helping to print handbills. He remembered sitting by her bed when she was sick, listening to her quiet voice and watching her face as she talked to him about things he couldn't hope to understand.

Softly but aloud he said, "Homesick," and saying it made him feel a little foolish. Home sure hadn't been much since Ma died. He guessed he missed Will Smith and his printing shop and newspaper office most of all.

Jed swung one boot up to the wagon wheel and looked around at the camp. The tents and huts reached toward the north in a great semicircle. The place looked almost pretty now in the red light of evening with the flicker of a cooking fire here and there, but Jed had seen enough of it to know that it was an endless sea of mud trampled by countless feet. The tents were torn and the men were sick from waiting to move on.

Beside the nearest tent four men stood around a cooking fire. They were warming something over it in a big can, and they huddled around, taking the warmth of the fire against the chill in the evening air. Jed looked along the row of wagons and saw some Negro teamsters gathering by a stack of barrels. Past them the wagon horses were strung out and blanketed for the night. There was a great soft hum over the camp, the muffled sounds of soldiers talking and swearing, and the sound of restless hoofs and jingling harnesses.

Now the teamsters were stirring and Jed heard one of them plucking the strings of a banjo. A voice broke clear on the damp cold air. The man sang a song that was strange to Jed, and its sadness and beauty reached

11

into him and made him glad to be alive. The other teamsters joined the singer in a rough background harmony, and Jed sat on the wagon and listened until it was dark. When the singing stopped he slid off the wagon and jumped into the mud. His boots sucked along as he walked to his tent, and his mind turned to Jim. Jed had shared a dog tent with Jim ever since Shiloh, and now Jim was lying sick.

When Jed came to their little tent he pulled back the poncho that was draped over the end and ducked in. Jim was sleeping soundly, his tall thin body stretched the length of the tent. He was nearly a head taller than Jed.

Jed pulled his overcoat out from under the blankets and put it on and lay down. He could feel the rough timber that they had thrown down to keep the mud

from coming up into the blankets. He listened to Jim's breathing for signs of pneumonia, but it seemed to be normal enough.

Jed knew that Jim had saved his life during the fight in the peach orchard. Instead of lying flat to the fire from Rebel rifles as he should have done, Jed knelt behind a tree to load and fire. A lot of Yankee soldiers even greener than Jed and not even knowing how to fire their rifles had bunched up behind him. Jim was nearby and he looked for Jed. He could see that the big knot of boys was drawing heavy fire. He tried to yell to Jed to get out of there and lie flat, but the thunder of battle was so loud that Jed didn't hear. Jim got up and ran over and grabbed him with one long arm and pulled him to the ground. They yelled at the other boys to lie flat too, but most of them were frozen with fear. No sooner had Jed started firing again than a shell hit the tree and blew it asunder. The tree wasn't big enough to protect one man, much less a whole bunch, and most of them were killed.

After the battle, when Jed tried to thank Jim, he just shrugged it off but it was a wonder to Jed that, tall as Jim was, he hadn't been riddled with bullets as soon as he'd got up off the ground.

Now Jim stirred in his blankets. "Where you been, Jed?" he asked in a sleepy voice.

"Thought you were sleeping," Jed said. "I just went

to the mess tent for a bite of food and then I went for a little walk."

"Did you have a dandy walk in this place of great beauty?" Jim asked.

"I surely did," Jed said. "I watched the sun set behind the snow-capped mountains and the cows coming down the hillside from their pasture."

"A lovely sight," said Jim with a little chuckle. "It must have been a very long walk indeed."

Their joke set Jed to dreaming again. Sometimes he and Jim had talked about taking a trip to the Far West when the War was over. Maybe if they talked some more about it Jim's spirits would perk up a little.

"Jim," he said. Jim didn't stir and Jed realized that he'd gone off to sleep again. Jed wished he felt like sleeping. He knew that Sergeant Charlie would be calling him for picket duty before dawn next morning.

From across the camp Jed heard the sound of taps and when the last mournful note had died away he shut his eyes.

He thought back to Elkhorn again and his pa and Will. Poor old kind-eyed Pa had married again after Ma was gone, and his new wife Nell bossed him without mercy until the day he died.

Will Smith was the only person Jed could go back to now. "When the War is over," Will had said, "come back here and stay with me. Being a widower I've got plenty of room over the shop. You can pick right up where you left off. You're the best printer's devil I ever had and when you get back I'd like you to do some writing too. I'm thinking of getting into politics and I'll be needing you."

Jed not only worked around the shop and turned the big wheel of the drum cylinder press but he ran errands for Will.

On Saturdays he and Will delivered papers in Delavan and Darien. *The Independent* was a weekly and it served people for miles around.

Jed remembered the fun of starting off on spring mornings when the air was soft as thistledown. He harnessed the horses and brought the wagon around to the front of the building and Will put a couple of

boxed lunches under the seat. They each loaded a bundle of papers before Will put up the tailboard. Then Will would lift his little dog Brownie into the wagon. Brownie would run around and put his paws up on the side and look over but when they started rolling he would sit up near the front with just his head sticking over, looking alert and serious.

When Will talked it was mostly about politics or maybe he would tell Jed stories about old Chief Blackhawk or Chief Bigfoot who used to roam the woodlands and prairies thereabouts.

When they left the papers at the hotels Will always stopped awhile to talk to his friends. Sometimes he talked so long that Jed got restless and took Brownie for a run or went to a store to buy a little paper bag of horehound candy. But Will was a good talker when he got going and mostly Jed just stayed and listened.

In the afternoon on the way home they stopped by a heavy wooden bridge and fished in Turtle Creek. Will let down the tailboard and got out his rod and Brownie hopped down and began sniffing around in the underbrush for rabbits.

Will frowned and chose a fly from his old soft hat and tied it to the leader. No man could fish that place better than Will, but his bad leg made him slow to move when a trout took the fly. That was where Jed came in. His bare legs would flash in the bright moving water and his quick brown hand would tighten over the handle of the net and trap the fish before it could shake itself free. Then Will would smile and throw the fish far out on the coarse green grass where Brownie would yelp at it, jumping back and pretending to be frightened and then jumping forward again as the fish flopped itself to death.

One day when the fishing was extra good Will said, "Good thing we don't notch our belts every time we catch a trout. We'd soon have nothing to hold up our pants."

If Jed brought fish home Nell gave a stiff little smile, but when he came home empty-handed she scowled and griped about how he never stayed home Saturdays to help with the chores.

No love was lost between Nell and Jed. When Pa died, Jed couldn't wait to join the Army even though he had to tell a kind of white lie about his age.

One of the other recruits told him a trick to use. This boy took a pencil and marked the figure 18 on a scrap of paper and told Jed to put it in his shoe. "When they ask you how old you are," he said, "just say you're over 18."

Jed knew he was lying — but the trick made him feel a little better anyway. When they got their new uniforms and rifles, Jed felt like quite a dandy. Nothing seemed so good as soldiering, except when the newness of their uniforms made other soldiers yell "Fresh fish" at them in a cackling chorus as they marched together down a company street.

Now it was pitch-dark in the tent and the sounds of the camp were fading in Jed's ears. He touched the stock of his rifle to make sure it was there beside him and he fell asleep.

CHAPTER TWO

THE next thing Jed knew, someone was shaking him awake. Dimly he saw the big face of Sergeant Charlie behind the lantern Charlie carried. "Wake up," Charlie said. "You got five minutes to get to the willow tree."

Jed loaded his rifle and stumbled through the dark to the mess tent and reached deep into a wooden box for some hardtack biscuits. Cookie was sleeping right beside the boxes and barrels of food. He was the best mess sergeant in camp and the kindest too, but if anyone tried to steal food from his stores they soon found out he was a light sleeper. He groaned and rolled over. "You goin' on picket duty, boy?" he asked.

"That's right, Cookie," Jed said.

"No hot coffee this early," Cookie said. "Come back when you've finished your duty."

Jed took the biscuits out front and broke them up with the butt of his rifle. The boys made plenty of jokes about hardtack. There was one joke going around camp about a sergeant who said, "Boys, I was eating a piece of hardtack this morning, and I bit into something soft. What do you think it was?"

One of the soldiers asked him, "Was it a worm?"

"No," said the sergeant. "It was a tenpenny nail."

As Jed chewed the hunks of biscuit he thought, This batch of hardtack really does feel harder than tenpenny nails.

He walked toward the willow tree where he was to stand guard, and he realized that the air was milky with fog. He was numb with dampness and cold, and the hardtack settled in a little wad in his stomach and made him feel almost hungrier than he had before. When he was first in the Army he used to torture himself by thinking of fresh eggs cooked on a griddle, or a plate of hot, steaming corn and new potatoes and a nice fat turkey leg, but lately he'd learned to keep his mind off such things.

Jed walked past the rows of silent tents. Once he banged into the corner of a tent at the end of a row, and he could feel his foot hit against one of the soldiers inside. The man groaned and cursed and was still.

Jed walked past the wagons and hospital tents. Once in a while a horse would snort or stamp his hoof, but aside from that, things were quiet. He walked across a soggy meadow that sometimes served as a parade ground and out toward the big willow tree. The tree seemed to come toward him suddenly out of the milky darkness and the boy standing under it wheeled around when he heard Jed coming. The boy couldn't have been much older than Jed. He was thin and he looked frightened. "Laws, you scared me," he said. "Didn't think it would be time for my relief to come just yet."

Jed smiled. "Well, it is," he said. "I bet you're glad to be finished with this lonely, thankless job."

"I am," the other boy said, "but I wish I was going back to my bed in Illinois 'stead of a mess of wet blankets."

"Cheer up," Jed said. "This war is bound to end someday."

"There are times when I think it will last a hundred years," the boy said.

"Wonder why they have us stand guard here," Jed said, trying to talk the boy out of his sadness. "I can't imagine a cavalry charge coming across that swampland."

"Neither can I," said the boy, "but I don't like it here, especially in a fog. Just before you came some poor beast must have fallen prey to an owl. I heard a most pitiful crying out there. It sounded almost

human, and when it stopped a chill went straight through me."

"You go on back and get some sleep," Jed said.

"What's your name?" the boy asked.

"Jed."

"Well, good night, Jed," the boy said, "and take care."

A place like this held no visions of Sleepy Hollow goblins for Jed. Living on the edge of a wilderness as he had back in Wisconsin, he'd learned to know the meanings of the sounds of night. But toward the end of the third hour of his watch, he heard a sound that shouldn't have been there. It was the sound of a dog whimpering. Jed walked slowly toward the sound, keeping his rifle at his side. When the sound stopped, Jed stopped and waited. When he heard it he moved forward. He went through brambles that tore at his trousers and coat.

Jed found the dog in a thicket not a hundred yards from the willow tree. The dog howled a little at first and as Jed walked up to him he growled. Jed knelt down beside him. "You sure look a lot like Brownie," he said, and put his hand under the warm chin and scratched a little. Then he scratched behind the soft ears, and the dog nuzzled Jed's hand and looked up at him with sad, friendly eyes and his tail thumped the

24

ground once. Jed figured he didn't have his full growth yet. His paws looked big.

Jed was so happy that he almost forgot he was on duty and that Sergeant Charlie would be coming around to check the pickets before the bugle sounded. The fog had thinned to a mist and there was just enough light so that Jed could study the dog's paws. He found what he was looking for right away. There was a big thorn in one paw and blood was coming out around it. Besides that, Jed could see that the poor thing was just tuckered out. He would have to rest before he started hunting his way home.

The dog shivered and Jed patted his brown-and-black-flecked side. It seemed to him that the ribs stuck out a mite more than they should.

Jed took the lame paw gently in one hand. With the thumb and middle finger of his other hand he grasped the thorn and pulled quickly and firmly. The thorn came out and blood gushed after it. Jed had never seen such a big thorn. The dog didn't make a sound. He just looked up at Jed, and Jed imagined that his eyes showed thanks. Jed reached up and untied his kerchief and wrapped it around the paw to soak up the blood and maybe keep out the dirt. He knew the kerchief wouldn't do much good but it seemed he had to do something. He gave the dog one more

25

pat and a longing look. "Hope you'll be ready to travel soon," he said. In his heart he knew he hoped the dog wouldn't travel, at least not yet.

He went back to the willow tree and listened. He wished he would hear just one little whimper, but he didn't hear a thing until the quick rousing notes of the bugle broke the air. After reveille he could hear the shouts of the sergeants as they woke the men, and once in a while an angry defiant shout from one of the waking soldiers.

CHAPTER THREE

RIGHT after reveille Sergeant Charlie came around. "Well, Jed," Charlie said, "did you break up any Rebel raids this morning?"

"Only a little one," Jed said. "How does it happen you didn't come around before this?"

"Now, I'm sorry, Jed," Charlie said. "If I'd a knowed it would worry you so I'd have come around earlier."

"I'll forgive you just this once," Jed said. "But don't let it happen again."

Charlie smiled and walked toward the next picket.

Jed heard Charlie whistling a little tune. Almost as soon as the sound of Charlie's whistling died away Jed heard something else. At first he thought it might be the dog working his way out of the thicket, but he soon realized that a little dog couldn't make that much noise.

Jed curled his finger around the trigger of his rifle and stood stock-still, trying to see into the waves of light, rolling mist that veiled the lowland. For a minute he heard nothing, and then he heard the crackle of dead branches and a crash as if someone had fallen down.

"Halt!" Jed called. "Who is that out there?"

There was no answer.

"Come forward and make yourself known," Jed called, "or I'll start shooting."

Then a voice spoke up. It was a child's voice. "Go ahead, Yankee," the voice said.

Jed lowered his rifle. "You come out here fast," he yelled.

There was no answer. Jed held his rifle loosely in one hand and moved forward. It came to him that maybe this was some kind of trap. He found his way to where the dog had been, but he wasn't there any more. He stood listening. Suddenly the dog began to yelp. Jed moved forward, following the sound. He went through the thicket to a little clearing on the other side. There he saw a young boy sitting on a log and looking mad enough to chew nails. He was bareheaded, his hair was the color of corn silk and his eyes were blue. The little dog was sitting at his feet and didn't make a sound as Jed walked up.

"What are you doing here?" Jed asked him.

The boy tilted his tan face up to Jed and looked at him with pure hate in his eyes. "Nothin' that matters to you," he said. "I woke up early and went out with my dog."

"It matters plenty to me," Jed said. "You should stay clear of this camp. It's lucky you didn't get shot."

"I need no Yankee mercy, soldier," the boy said.

Jed could feel himself getting hot under the collar. "You mind your tongue, boy," he said. "There are pickets all around this camp and some of them have itching trigger fingers."

"I hate Yankees," the boy said, "and most of all I hate Yankee soldiers. My pa's a Confederate soldier."

"Then I don't blame you for hating Yankee soldiers," Jed said, "but there's no call to get yourself shot to prove it."

He looked down at the blond head and at the dog sitting trustingly by the boy's feet. "Now you get up and cut out of here as fast as your legs will carry you," he said. "I go off duty soon and you'd best not be here when the next man comes around."

The dog got up and limped toward Jed, wagging his tail and looking up. He leaned down and gave the dog a pat. "Now take your dog and git," he said. "Walk straight out that way. Don't circle around or you're liable to get shot by one of the other pickets."

The boy sat on the log, not saying a word or making a move. Finally he said, "I can't walk. I fell in a chuckhole and when I walk my leg near kills me."

Jed faced the boy, holding his rifle in one hand, his other hand in a fist on his hip. He gazed at him thoughtfully.

"How far do you live from here?" he asked.

"Two or three miles I guess," the boy said, "but I'm not likely to tell you which way. You'd bring those other Yankees around to steal our pigs and chickens and burn our buildings."

"Well, you can't crawl home," Jed said. "Maybe your leg is broken. I better take you to our surgeon and get him to fix you up."

"If you're a mind to shoot me," the boy said, "shoot

me here. No use to drag me back to that Yankee camp."

Jed found it hard to keep a straight face. "Now don't be a fool," he said. "Even Yankees don't shoot children."

He moved forward and reached out his hand so the boy could hang on and hop to the willow tree. "Come on," he said, "there's no use fighting me."

The boy drew back his hand. "Not while there's a breath in me," he said.

Jed turned on his heel. "You can't go far on a broken leg," he said, "and I don't have the heart to leave a tad like you to starve. You think things over. I'll come back later to see if you've changed your mind."

He walked back to the willow tree and looked around and listened and settled back against the tree.

His relief came about half an hour later when the sun had burned the mist away and stood like a red ball in the east.

"Well, how you been, Davy?" Jed asked the boy.

"Fine, Jed boy," his relief said. "I thought maybe you died of the fever, I haven't seen you for so long."

Davy was no taller than Jed, but he was thicker, and he had a bullet-shaped head. Jed looked him up and down. "I have a fever that makes me ache to get out of here and fight this war to a finish," he said.

31

"You ain't just waggin' your tongue, Jed boy," Davy said. "Most anything is better than this."

Jed hesitated and looked into Davy's eyes. "Davy," he said.

"What is it, boy?" Davy asked.

"Well, it might be hard to believe," Jed said, suddenly talking very fast, "but there's a little boy out there past that thicket. He's hurt his leg and I got to take him to the surgeon to get him fixed up. Maybe the surgeon can figure out a way to get him home without kicking up a fuss with Captain Pike and all. I'd like it if you could keep this a secret."

"Why, all right," Davy said. "How old is the boy?"

"'Bout eight or nine I guess," Jed said. "I haven't heard him stir since I found him, so he must still be there."

"Maybe it's some trick," Davy said.

"I thought of that," Jed said, "but I can't figure out what kind of trick it would be. Anyway I don't think he's play-acting."

"Well, go ahead and get him," Davy said. "If it was me I'd let the little Rebel crawl back home."

"Now you don't mean that, surely," Jed said.

CHAPTER FOUR

THE boy was sitting on the same log but now his dog was in his lap. Jed went over and scratched the dog's ear. "He sure is a nice little hound," he said. "Reminds me of a dog back home."

The boy looked down at the dog's paw. "I reckon that's your kerchief," he said.

"Wasn't worth a hang," Jed said. He looked down and shifted his feet. "What's your name anyway?" he asked.

"Philip," the boy said.

"Are you coming with me, Philip? If your leg is broken someone better set it for you."

"If my pa ever knew I went into a Yankee camp he'd die of shame." The boy sat there for a minute patting his dog. "Better not let my pa ketch you," he said. "He can shoot a wood tick off a log at fifty paces."

"That's some shootin'," Jed said. "Now come along with me."

The boy put his dog down and stood up on one foot and grabbed Jed's arm for support. He gave Jed a long look and then he stuck his lower lip out and all of a sudden shoved Jed so hard he nearly lost his balance. "I just can't go with a Yankee," he said. "Leave me be."

Jed almost busted out laughing but then he looked down at the boy and he felt himself getting mad. Very slowly he took the bayonet off his rifle, stuck it into its scabbard and slung the rifle over his shoulder. He grabbed the boy under the arms and dragged him right through the brambles to the foot of the willow tree. The dog seemed to think it was some kind of game. He ran around them, yelping and growling and wagging his tail. The boy hit Jed a couple of times, then he grew quiet.

As they came to the foot of the tree Davy grinned. "Well, it looks like you got an ornery package there, Jed boy," he said, "and you didn't tell me about no dog."

"Do me a big favor and keep this dog here, Davy," Jed said. "I got my hands full, as you can see."

"You sure do," Davy said, "but I don't see why I

have to take care of that Rebel flea bag for that cussed boy."

"He's no flea bag," the boy said. "You leave him alone and let him come with me."

"He's a nice little dog," Jed said. "You keep him here for me, Davy. If we take him into camp, he'll only make a fuss."

"Hurry back," Davy said, reaching out for the dog's homemade leather collar.

As Jed half dragged, half helped the boy toward camp, the dog set up a pitiful crying and howling. Jed tried to soothe the boy. "He'll be right there when we get back," he said. He dragged the boy about ten paces more. "How about giving me a little help?" he asked.

The boy answered by giving a giant wrench to free himself and falling on the ground. Jed could feel the color draining out of his face. He leaned over and picked the boy off the ground and slung him over his shoulder like a sack of meal, letting his legs dangle down in front. "I should have let you stay there and rot," he said.

Davy had been watching the whole show. "You should hang him to a tree near his house for his ma to see," he called.

"Now that's takin' talk too far," Jed said. "Mind you take care of that little dog."

The hospital tents weren't too far from the willow

tree but it wasn't long before the boy began to feel heavy. Jed saw that a black horse with a long white streak down his nose was tethered to a pole near the surgeon's tent. "The doctor must be here," he said.

"Let me down now," the boy said. "I'll give you no more trouble."

Jed leaned forward and slid the boy gently onto his good leg. "I thought I had you tamed once before," he said. The boy took Jed's arm and hopped to the tent. "You sit out here on this crate," Jed said, "and wait till I have a chance to speak to the surgeon."

He pulled back the tent flap and went in. The surgeon was working at a folding desk. He didn't even look up when Jed came in. There was a litter of papers all around him, and half a dozen candle stubs lay on the floor. He was a small man with curly black hair and a little pointed beard on his chin. His overcoat was thrown around his shoulders, and his jacket was open at the neck.

Finally he looked up. "Hello," he said. "I thought you were my orderly. Come back in half an hour if you want treatment, and go to the tent at the other end of the row." He smiled a tired smile. "Looks as if you might last that long."

"It's not for me I'm here, sir," Jed said. "I have a little boy outside. He's hurt his leg. His father is a Confederate soldier and he didn't want to come here, but he couldn't get home by himself, and I couldn't leave him out there to starve."

"Out where, son?" the surgeon asked.

"Out past a big willow tree where I was standing guard," Jed said. "He told me he woke up early and went out with his dog. He's not afraid of the devil himself."

37

"Do you have another picket in your place?" the surgeon asked.

"Yes, sir," Jed said. "My relief is out there now."

The surgeon looked past Jed toward the tent flap. This time his smile was broader than before. "Is that the boy?" he asked.

Jed turned and saw the boy's head sticking through the opening. "It's nobody else, sir," he said and reached out his hand and helped the boy into the tent.

"I have a boy about your age," the surgeon said. "Let me see that leg, son."

The boy scowled and put his chin down. "I'm no Yankee general's son," he said.

The surgeon looked at the boy pleasantly and laughed. "I wish I were a general," he said. "Now let me see that leg."

The boy pulled up his trouser leg and showed a shin all black and blue. "It hurts like the mischief when I try to stand on it," he said.

The surgeon came around from behind his table, knelt down and ran his fingers up and down the bone. "It's broken," he said. "I'll set it and put a splint on it. Soldier," he said to Jed, "what's your company commander's name?"

"Captain Pike, sir," Jed said.

"You go tell him what's happened," the surgeon said, "and ask him if he can give you a couple of horses and another man so's you can take this lad back home when I've finished with him. He shouldn't walk on this leg."

"I hope you'll pardon me for saying it," Jed said, "but Captain Pike is a mean cuss. I'd like to take the boy back myself. It may be a lot to ask, but if I could just use your horse . . ."

"I can't let you do that, soldier," the surgeon said. "I can't take the responsibility for that."

He went back to his desk and sat down and scratched his beard. "What kind of a man is your sergeant?" he asked.

"Sergeant Charlie is a good man," Jed said. "If he says I can go, will you let me use your horse? I'll stay off the roads and keep a sharp lookout for Confederate patrols."

The surgeon turned to the boy. "Are any Confederate soldiers likely to be in your neighborhood?" he asked. "This man is doing you a service. I'd hate to have him get shot." Then he smiled. "And I can't afford to lose my horse," he said.

"Not that I know of," the boy said. "'Cept for my pa I haven't seen a soldier since the War started. Until today, that is. And there are no roads between here and our house, just swampland and woods. Only person that might shoot him is my ma."

"I doubt that your ma will shoot him under the

circumstances," the surgeon said. He turned to Jed. "You go back and tell Sergeant Charlie where you're going. And tell him the less said about this the better."

"I will," Jed said, "and I'll stop by for some coffee and salt pork while I'm at it. I got nothing but hardtack before I went on duty this morning."

"Hardtack's about as good for a man as pasteboard," the surgeon said.

CHAPTER FIVE

A S Jed walked into camp he could feel a faint
warmth from the morning sun. Some of the men,
having nothing better to do, were sitting around talking or whittling or playing cards.

Jed thought how much spunk that pesky little
sandy-haired tad seemed to have and he thought about
the soft-eared, big-eyed little dog that looked so much
like Brownie.

He walked past a couple of men sitting outside their
tent trying to soak up some sunshine. One of them had
a full beard, and his cap was jammed down over one
eye at a cocky angle. One of the other men said something that Jed couldn't hear.

"He sure is a young 'un," said the man with the
beard.

Jed turned and gave them his toughest, hardest look

and walked on past, but he nearly tripped over a tent rope. He had to catch his balance so he wouldn't go sprawling in the mud.

He walked up to the mess tent. Cookie had already given out breakfast. "What you comin' around here for now, Jed?" he said. "Don't expect no handouts from me."

Jed smiled at him. "Cookie, you know I have more sense than to ask you for handouts," he said. "Don't you remember I came around and stole some hardtack before dawn this morning and you told me to come back when I finished picket duty and get some coffee?"

"Laws," Cookie said, "I forgot all about that. I didn't know you'd been on duty. Sit down there on that barrel and I'll give you some hot coffee." He lowered his voice. "And a little fresh pork."

"Where the devil did you get fresh pork?" Jed asked. "I thought the countryside was about played out. I didn't think there was a pig left within fifteen miles of here."

"Shhh, now never you mind," Cookie said. "If I give you some, will you keep your mouth shut?"

"Except when I'm eating it," Jed said.

"You're fresh as paint," said Cookie.

Jed looked over at him. Mess is a good name for him, he thought as he swallowed some of the bitter coffee and looked at Cookie's uniform pants so stained

with grease that they were nearer black than light blue. But Jed knew it was lucky they had Cookie in their company. Most mess sergeants were such bad cooks that the men just got their daily ration and cooked it themselves, but Cookie took pleasure in cooking and he was a worker. His heart was even bigger than his stomach. But it took more than a big heart to feed a regiment, and the way things were going now it looked as if they might be eating tree roots by Christmas.

When Cookie wasn't looking, Jed folded the piece of pork and slipped it into his pocket for Jim to nibble in case he'd missed breakfast.

No sooner had he hidden the pork than Cookie gave him another slice. Jed thanked him and went over and fished a couple of hardtack biscuits out of the box and sat back down.

He nibbled at the hardtack and munched the pork. The taste of the pork made him think of the times when there had been food to spare. When they'd first made camp in this place, their soldiers had gone out to forage at the big plantations nearby. They brought back pigs and chickens and smoked hams and sometimes even cows on the hoof. When Cookie got finished with some of that stuff, it was better than any food Jed had ever tasted. But it always seemed a little tainted somehow.

Once Jed had gone with a gang of soldiers to forage at a plantation. He found he had no stomach for that kind of thing. Forage was just another word for steal.

Most of the people on the plantations were boys too young to fight or women and slaves. Some of the younger slaves had run away to the North, trying to

44

find jobs to help the armies that they hoped would bring freedom to their people.

Sergeant Charlie had told Jed and another boy to stand guard while the other soldiers loaded a wagon with livestock and food. Jed felt like a coward, guarding soldiers from slaves that stood helpless and frightened, and women and children who huddled in a tight, bitter knot and watched while their food was carted off.

The dogs howled and barked around them, and Jed had to knock down another boy's rifle so he wouldn't shoot one of them. "Have some pity," Jed said. "Don't shoot their dogs."

Jed knew that some Yankee soldiers had treated Southerners much rougher than they had, burning their barns and sometimes even their houses, but Jed knew that unless he was ordered to go he'd have to be starving before he'd go raiding again.

Jed popped the last morsel of fresh pork into his mouth with a corner of hardtack biscuit and put the other biscuit into his pocket. He was just about to stand up and go to the tent to see how Jim was faring, when Sergeant Charlie came along. Charlie sniffed the air and grinned at Cookie. "I see you're treating my pickets nice and kind," he said. "Now it seems funny to me that there was no smell of pork at breakfast this morning."

45

"Nor will there be at dinner," Cookie said.

Charlie moved forward and held out his hand. "Just a little piece now, Cookie, so's the whole regiment won't find out about it."

"If I didn't like you, Charlie," Cookie said, handing Charlie a slice of pork, "I'd give you nothing. You can tell the whole army I have fresh pork for all I care. I've been keeping that pig under my cot for two months trying to fatten him up. Yesterday I gave it up and today we have a little pork."

Charlie laughed and started off. "Got to go see Captain Pike," he said.

Jed got up from the barrel. "Charlie," he said, "I got to speak to you in private about something that happened while I was on picket duty this morning."

"All right," Charlie said, "I'll walk you back to your tent."

Jed turned to Cookie. "Thanks for taking care of my needs, Cookie," he said.

They walked away from the mess tent. Sergeant Charlie shoved his big hands deep into his overcoat pockets and hunched over. "Well now, Jed," he said, "what's on your mind this morning?"

Jed told Charlie about finding the boy and about taking him to the surgeon. He told him he could use the surgeon's horse to take the boy back home. As he talked Charlie's face grew set and hard. "I guess I better tell Captain Pike your story and let him decide what we should do," he said. "Something like this could get us into a mess o' trouble."

"I'm more than glad to take him myself," Jed said, "and the surgeon says the less fuss the better."

"I see his point there," Charlie said kicking a stone toward a tree stump. He lowered his voice. "And Captain Pike being somewhat cantankerous maybe we'd better handle this ourselves." He looked hard at Jed. "Mind you keep out of trouble and look sharp for Rebel patrols."

"I will," Jed said, "but I doubt that I'll see any. The boy says he's seen no Rebel soldiers about, and I believe he's telling the truth, pesky as he's been."

Charlie pursed his lips. "I've got to go over and talk to Captain Pike now. He says he wants to get us back in shape. Sounds to me as if we might be moving out of here soon."

"Can't be too soon to suit me," Jed said.

"Me either," Charlie said, "but the big trouble is that more than half our men are down sick."

"Jim is sick right now," Jed said, "and I want to go back and see him before I leave."

"No wanderin' around tomorrow," Charlie said. "Captain Pike wants us all to drill." Charlie tried to make his mouth into a thin line like Captain Pike's, and he pushed his nose flat. "Good drilling makes good soldiers," he said in a nasal voice.

Jed brought his heels together so fast he almost fell over. He gave Charlie a mock salute. "Yessir," he said.

Jed walked over and ducked into their tent. Jim was sitting up but looking kind of miserable.

"How you feeling, Jim?" Jed asked.

"Better," he said. "How was picket duty this morning?"

"Chilly," Jed said. "Did you get some breakfast?"

"Sure did," said Jim. "A saintly-looking woman in a starched white apron came tripping up to me with a silver tray with a pot of fresh-made coffee on it and two eggs fried in butter and three fresh slices of oatmeal bread and a little pot of gooseberry jam. There was a nice white napkin made into a tent sitting on the side of the tray. It was like a breakfast I had in a big hotel once."

"Now you spoiled it," Jed said. "I believed it all

48

till you got to the napkin." He looked down at Jim. "No fooling, Jim," he said, "we got to get some food into you."

He reached into his pocket for the slice of pork. "Eat this," he said. "Cookie gave it to me."

Jim took a bite and munched on it. "Thanks, old partner," he said. "What would I do without you?"

"You'd go to the hospital where you belong," Jed said.

"If I went to the hospital," said Jim, "I'd sicken and die." He took a kerchief out of his pocket and wrapped up the pork he hadn't eaten. "I'll keep this awhile," he said. He looked at a little slice of blue sky at the end of the tent. "Throw back that poncho and let's have a game of checkers. We haven't played checkers for quite a spell."

"I can't play right now. I've got to straighten out something that happened when I was on picket duty this morning."

"What happened?" Jim asked.

"A boy and his dog wandered in from a nearby farm. The boy broke his leg and the surgeon's fixing him up. I have to take him home."

Right away Jim looked worried and Jed wished he hadn't told him.

"I'll go along with you," Jim said, though he must

have known he wouldn't have the strength to walk across camp.

Jed just smiled. "You got to stay here and get your strength back. There's no danger or I wouldn't be going alone. I won't follow roads."

"I don't like the sound of it," Jim said.

Jed took off his coat and stuffed it into his blankets. "Don't you worry," he said. "I've been doing some worrying about you though. Go over and get yourself some food. Cookie will give you something if he knows you were too sick to eat any breakfast."

"Well, mind you don't get yourself into any trouble now," Jim said.

CHAPTER SIX

A T one end of the low row of hospital tents a group of men were waiting to see the orderly. Doubtless many of them were really sick and would have to see the surgeon, but some had nothing better to do than play "old soldier."

As Jed walked toward the surgeon's tent, one of the men yelled at him to fall in and wait his turn.

"I got business with the surgeon," Jed said, and kept on walking.

He thought, I hope I can trust that boy to take me straight to his house and not get me into trouble. I don't think he has a mite of bad in him when it comes to that.

Inside, he found the boy sitting on a box patiently waiting.

"Well, it's set and ready," the surgeon said. "Did Sergeant Charlie give you leave to take him home?"

"Yes sir, he did," Jed said. "He said we better handle this ourselves."

"Are there any men waiting outside the orderly's tent?" the surgeon asked.

"Yes, there are," said Jed.

"I'll tell him to herd them inside. Then we'll put the lad on my horse, and you can be on your way. I'll tell the orderly to leave his horse for me to use so's you won't have to break your neck getting back here."

While the surgeon was gone, the boy gave Jed a shy smile. "That's one good doctor," he said.

When the surgeon came back he and Jed took the boy outside and hoisted him as gently as they could to the horse's back. Then Jed mounted and patted the coal-black neck. "He sure is a beauty," he said. "I'll take good care of him."

The surgeon held Jed's rifle. "I better keep this for you," he said. He took off his pistol and handed it up to Jed. "This might come in handy. The rifle would only be in your way."

"Thank you, sir," said Jed. "I got to make room for a dog on here too."

The surgeon rolled his eyes to the sky in a gesture of despair. "A dog too?" he said. "Can't he walk behind?"

"His foot's hurt," Jed said. "I got a big thorn out of it awhile back."

"If kindness could win a war," the surgeon said, "you could win one singlehanded."

"Take a tight grip on my belt," Jed said to the boy. "I don't want you falling off and breaking your other leg."

As they moved across the field the boy didn't say a word, but as soon as he saw his dog he started talking to him. The dog broke away from Davy and limped over, wagging his tail and kicking up a happy fuss by the side of the horse.

"I suppose you're going out and get shot for that little Rebel there," Davy said. He walked over and handed the dog up and Jed took him. The dog squirmed and wriggled, trying to get back to the boy.

"Can you hold my belt with one hand and the dog with the other?" Jed asked.

"I can do that," the boy said. Jed handed him the dog and the boy held him in the crook of his arm.

Jed looked down at Davy. "If I'm not back when your relief comes, tell him I'll be coming back through this way," Jed said, "and don't tell a living soul about this boy."

"How come you want to get in the good graces of a Rebel family, Jed boy?" Davy asked, making his eyes into little slits. "Maybe you think they might fatten you up a little. That it?"

Jed was getting sick to death of Davy. "See you later," he said, and they started off into the swampy thicket.

"If you want to keep things quiet," Davy called, as if it was the biggest joke in the world, "bring me a side of bacon or maybe a barrel of apples."

"I'll bring you a whole railroad car filled with apples," Jed yelled. Then softly, almost under his breath, he said, "Crab apples would be too good for a cuss like that."

"He's a Yankee soldier," the boy said. "How come you don't like him?"

"Now that's a fool question," Jed said, and he

jammed his cap down on his head so the branches wouldn't knock it off.

They went through a place so swampy that Jed began to fear that the horse would start sinking and never stop. "Now which way?" he asked the boy.

"The fog was thick when I came here," the boy said, "but if we just keep going we should get to a stream and we can follow it."

Jed was beginning to have his doubts about the boy's sense of direction, but he kept urging the horse along until they came to a stream that wandered through the swampy land.

"Follow the stream that way," the boy said, pointing west. "I'll tell you where to cross over."

Jed could feel the boy's hand tighten on his belt.

"My dog doesn't like it much up here," he said. "This is the first time he's ever been up on a horse."

Jed kept a sharp lookout ahead to be sure that they stayed on as high ground as possible. The stream cut sharply into the soft earth and here, though the land was low and nasty, it was passable. Sometimes there were no banks at all, and the stream spilled into formless, swampy pools. Jed had to guide the horse carefully around great reddish vines that hung from the trees, and sometimes the undergrowth seemed almost more of a hazard than the uncertain ground.

Just when the going seemed almost impossible and Jed was about to ask the boy if he had the least idea where he was, the land began to rise. The woods seemed more pleasant and the undergrowth not so thick.

Jed went slow and steady to keep the boy from falling. Now the ground grew firm under the horse's hoofs, the saddle creaked pleasantly, and sunlight filtered through the overhanging branches. Until now Jed hadn't known how sick he'd grown of the life in camp. Camp was like a cold little island in the middle of enemy territory. Out here the smell and noise of men hadn't driven away every living thing.

They hadn't been traveling long when just past a bend in the stream Jed could see a place that looked like a good crossing.

"This is where we cross," the boy said.

Jed let the horse stop for a drink. He sat easy in the saddle. "This is a pretty place," he said, looking down into the clear shallow water.

"Before my pa went off to war," the boy said, "he used to bring me here and we'd sit on that far bank and he'd tell me stories. He's as good a storyteller as ever was. And sometimes when he smoked a pipe he'd blow rings for me. Those rings were as round as a plate or a bowl."

"Is that why you came here?" Jed asked. "Because you used to come here with your pa?"

When the boy didn't answer, Jed turned around and looked at him. His eyes had a faraway look in them as if he might be trying to understand what it meant to be a soldier. "Do you think my pa will come back safe and sound?" he asked.

Jed looked back down at the water. He studied the tips of the ripples made silver by the sunlight. He looked at the sandy bottom and the outlines of the little stones blurred by the moving water. "I hope with all my heart he will," he said.

CHAPTER SEVEN

THE horse raised his head and shook it and gave a happy, satisfied snort. "Want a drink?" Jed asked the boy.

"Guess I can hold out till we get home," he said. "The next part's easy and I know it well."

"How in tarnation did you get from here to that willow tree?" Jed asked. "You must have started before dawn."

"I did," the boy said. "When Pa was home he always got up before daylight to do the chores and sometimes I got up and helped him. If we finished in good time and the weather was warm we'd come down here to fish. Dark or light it's all the same to me. But this morning my dog took a scent and he ran into the woods and I tailed him. The little devil wouldn't come back to me no matter how much I called. Then the fog settled down and I lost my direction for a spell. Ma says I better get busy at trainin' this dog or he'll just be a worthless hound."

Jed urged the horse up the bank, and they followed the stream on the other side. The ground kept rising and growing drier, and the stream got deeper and narrower and there were more rocks in its bed.

"You ever fish back home?" the boy asked.

"You bet your life," Jed said. "I fished with a friend of mine. He had a dog just like yours."

There was a long silence as they rode along the stream, and then the boy said, "I'm sorry for the things I said, and I'm sorry for hitting you."

"Don't think about that," Jed said. "Just keep your eyes open for signs of trouble."

"I'll do that," the boy said.

They moved through grasses and across open rocky places toward another wood, always keeping near the stream and using it as a guide. As they neared the edge of the woods they startled a big brown bird in the underbrush, and it went flapping away through the trees. "Likely a woodcock," said the boy.

They came out into a field that slanted upward to a ridge where the ripple of the grass blurred the line of the hill as it came against the sky.

"We live just over that hill," the boy said. "Pa thought it likely we'd be safer here than in a town."

59

The horse's legs swished through the grass, and Jed was struck by the silence and the beauty of the place. "No doubt your pa was right," he said.

As they moved toward the crest of the hill, a shot broke the stillness of the air. Jed jerked up straight. In the grass about a hundred yards beyond them a woman was standing in full view with a musket in her hands.

"It's Ma," the boy said.

Jed sat up straight and cupped his hands. "I got your boy here, ma'am," he yelled as loud as he could.

He saw the woman stretch up to look. Then she dropped her musket and came running down the hill. Jed turned the horse sideways so she could see that the boy was all right and not lying across the horse, as he would be if he'd been badly hurt.

After the boy's talk and the shooting, Jed expected the woman to be big and tough like Nell, but she was small and very pretty. She ran up to them and looked at the boy, not saying a thing, just trembling with fear and anger. Then she turned her head to look up

at Jed. "What is my son doing on a Yankee soldier's horse?" she asked. "You come down right now, Philip."

The woman was blond like her son. Her hair was done up in a knot at the back, and she wore a light blue woolen dress. She held her hand up to the boy. "Well, Philip," she said, "come on down. And as for you, Yankee," she said to Jed, "you better get back to your camp."

Jed could feel anger rising in him for the second time that day. "I'd better take him over the hill, ma'am," he said. "He's got a broken leg."

She walked around the horse and saw the splint and the bandage on the boy's leg. "Philip," she said, "you promised me you'd never go near that Yankee camp. Now you been in it. Now every one of those con-sarned Yankee freebooters will hightail it over here to wreck our place."

The boy just looked down at his ma and didn't say a word. Finally he said, "I went to a place by the stream where Pa and I used to go and then I got lost in a fog."

Jed could tell from the boy's voice that he was fighting back tears.

The woman looked at Jed. "I'll help Philip back to the house," she said. "Then we'll get ready to move out. We can't stay, with you all knowing we're here. All I ask is don't do any burning. You don't stand to gain from burning our buildings."

"I'll take him to the house, ma'am," Jed said, "and I doubt that you'll have to move out. Only my sergeant and my tentmate and the surgeon know about this, and I know they won't tell. Then there's my relief picket. He knows too. I already told him not to mention it, and when I get back I'll talk to him again to make sure."

Jed turned halfway around and looked at the boy and the dog. "And never fear that I'll tell, ma'am," he said. "I like your boy and the little dog too."

The woman's face softened. "How old are you, Yankee?" she asked with the ghost of a smile.

Jed looked down at the grass. He could feel himself blushing. He'd never seen such a pretty woman, and now she was talking to him as if she was his mother. He wanted to lie, but he couldn't. "Sixteen, ma'am," he said.

"Well, go ahead and take Philip to the house," she said, "and when I've got him settled I'll give you a bit of food and a mug of cider. After your kindness to Philip I guess I owe you that much."

Jed didn't know why, but that made him mad. "You owe me nothing, ma'am," he said, "and let me tell you something else. If you go around shooting at Yankee soldiers, you'll end up with your barn burned and your house too and the devil only knows what else. This is an ugly war. It's nothing short of a miracle that your place has gone untouched. Our soldiers have treated your country mighty rough, as well you know."

The woman looked off down the hill. "I know it was a fool-headed thing for me to fire that musket," she said. Then she looked down at the ground. "It seems you don't think so much of Yankee raids."

"I went raiding once, ma'am, and I didn't like it," Jed said, "but I don't know how we'd live if we didn't live off the land. Your raiders are playing the devil with our supply lines."

Anger flashed in the woman's eyes and she opened her mouth to speak, but then she thought better of it.

"Do me a favor, Yankee," the boy said, "and take me to the house. You and Ma can fight it out later. I'm getting saddlesore."

Jed chuckled and nudged the horse with his heel, and they walked slowly to the crest of the hill, where the woman picked up her musket. They went down a slope and skirted some trees, and there on a rise beyond the trees Jed saw one of the prettiest little farms he'd ever seen. The house itself was small. It was set on a fieldstone foundation, and its white clapboards reflected the sun, giving them the color of fresh butter. Off to the northwest there was an apple orchard and toward them, just out of the shadow of the trees, was a big gray, unpainted shed that served as a barn.

Beyond the barn someone had cultivated the corner of a field that stretched off to the south.

"You got a nice place here, ma'am," Jed said. "It's not like the big plantations I've seen hereabouts and elsewhere in the South. It reminds me of some of our farms back home."

"My husband loves this place," the woman said. "He was a schoolteacher before he joined up. He would be a doctor, but our money ran out before he finished his studies."

"That's a shame, ma'am," Jed said. "Doctors are sorely needed in times like these."

As they approached the house, Jed saw a girl in the doorway. She looked to be about fourteen as far as he could tell. "Is Philip all right, Ma?" she asked in a frightened voice.

"Broke his leg," the woman said, "but aside from that he's fine."

"Thank heaven it's no more than that," the girl said.

"This soldier has befriended him," said the woman. Jed noticed how much the girl looked like her ma except that her hair tumbled loose to her shoulders.

The girl went back into the house, and Jed and the boy's ma helped him down from the horse. Jed tethered the horse by the door.

"Let me sit on the step awhile, Ma," the boy said.

"It's warm in the sun today, and I don't want to play sick just yet."

"No need to play sick at all. Just keep off that leg," the woman said. She turned to Jed. "Would you like to have a look around before you go?" she asked.

By now the little hound seemed as good as new, and he wasn't content to stay with the boy. He frisked around Jed, and Jed knelt down to pat him. "I'd like to see your place," he said "A soldier doesn't realize how much he's missing until he gets away from camp for a while."

Jed looked up at the woman, and he saw the sadness in her smile. "I'll show you our barn first," she said.

CHAPTER EIGHT

JED stood in the doorway of the barn, breathing in the homely, comforting smells. Inside there were two horses and a skinny cow. The horses were dappled grays. Jed admired the powerful thighs and the feathered fetlocks and the big hoofs that had stamped the earth into a hard floor. "That's a beautiful pair of animals, ma'am," he said.

"Hate to think of bein' without Pete and Dan," she said. "You come from a farm, soldier?"

"Kind of a farm, ma'am. Back in Wisconsin."

They walked around to the side of the barn and Jed took a look inside the chicken house. "We had chickens at our place," he said, "but I never did learn to love the pesky things."

They stood by the pigpen and watched the antics of

67

the two pigs. One of them was younger than the other and he broke into a run and charged into the side of the older one, making him squeal and finally teasing him into a little play. Their snouts were reddish brown from foraging in the earth. Jed couldn't help thinking how short a time it would take a handful of soldiers to dispatch those pigs.

As they walked around, Jed noticed that, beautiful as the place was, it was badly in need of a man's labor. When they looked over the slope north of the house, he saw that part of one of the big apple trees had died and had been split off by the wind. It hung forlornly by a few splinters with its branches on the ground, waiting for someone to chop it up for firewood.

"You got an ax and a sledge and a couple of wedges, ma'am?" Jed asked. "Apple makes good firewood."

"No call for you to do our work," she said.

"Ma'am, I'll go to jelly if I don't do something. It won't take but a few minutes."

Jed hung his jacket on a branch of a tree and followed the woman to a dusky, pungent toolshed. She showed him the tools and he took them out and chopped away the dead part of the tree and chopped it up and split it into sections. It felt good to be bending his arms and back again, and when he stacked the wood, he could feel the sweat tingling on his body.

When Jed put his jacket on again, the woman came over and gave him a big mug of cool cider.

"That's as good as any cider I ever had," he said, "and we're proud of our cider back in Wisconsin."

He handed the mug back.

"Would you like some more?" the woman asked him.

"I appreciate your friendliness more than I can say," Jed said, "but now it's time for me to go. The horse belongs to our surgeon, and I can't keep him here forever."

Jed and the woman went back to the house. The boy was still sitting on the step. "You sure can make the chips fly," he said.

"When you live in Wisconsin, you got to know how to make chips fly," Jed said, looking down at the boy. "Well, I'll say good-by," he said. "Mind you stay off that leg until it's better, and keep away from Yankee camps."

Jed mounted the horse and looked down at the woman. "Don't worry about me telling the boys about your place," he said. "I won't tell another soul."

"Thank you, soldier," she said.

He nudged the horse and cantered back to the crest of the hill. He turned and looked back once. The woman and the boy were sitting on the doorstep, looking after Jed. The dog was the only one that was moving. He was at the pigpen, yelping around and bothering the pigs. He sure is a cute little cuss, Jed thought. He gave a little salute with his right hand and rode off across the hill through the tawny grass and into the woods.

He knew he'd been away longer than expected, and he didn't want to worry the surgeon, so whenever the underbrush thinned a little, he urged the horse along.

He crossed the stream where he and the boy had crossed and went through the woods and into the lowland.

When he was about a quarter of a mile from camp, he looked up at the sun and figured it must be about noon, so he let out a bellow. "Hey, Davy," he called.

Jed heard someone call back. He couldn't make out the words, but he went straight toward the green-and-gold-tipped branches of the willow which showed above the tops of the other trees. He called again when he came in closer, and Davy's voice answered. "Come on in, Jed boy."

When Jed pulled up to the tree, Davy looked up at the horse in mock disappointment. "Where's all that good food?" he asked, pulling the corners of his mouth into a grin.

Jed looked at Davy's face and all of a sudden he wanted to kick it. But he made himself answer softly. If Davy had any good in him, Jed had to find out where it was. "That boy lives on a small farm," he

70

said, "with his mother and sister. They probably have scarcely enough food to get them through the winter. The best thing we can do is forget we ever heard of the place."

Davy was still looking up. His expression hadn't changed. "Did they feed you up good, Jed boy?" he asked. "You sure were away a long time."

Jed knew he'd better go. If he got any sicker of Davy, he'd show his anger, and he knew that would be the worst thing he could do. "I didn't eat a morsel of their food," he said. "There's nothing worth taking. In case you might be thinking of going there," he said, pointing over the lowland, "that stretch of swamp is as nasty a piece of land as I've ever seen. It's snake country if I've ever seen any, and some of the bogs are so sticky if a man got into one it would drag him straight to hell."

Davy looked a little worried and then his eyes popped out and he puffed up his cheeks and let the air blow out of his mouth. He started cackling and laughing and slapping his knees. "Why, I never knew you were such a storyteller, Jed boy," he said between cackles. "You should come over to our cooking fire sometime and entertain the boys."

The blood rushed to Jed's face. He kicked the horse into a gallop and fastened his eyes on the tops of the hospital tents.

I believe that consarned ape means to raid that little farm, he thought.

As Jed galloped up, the surgeon came out of his tent. "Glad to see you back, son," he said. He looked into Jed's face. "Is it my imagination, or are you mad at someone?"

As Jed dismounted he had half a mind to tell the surgeon about Davy, but he figured the surgeon had enough to worry about. He handed over the surgeon's belt. "It's nothing," he said. "It's just that picket out there. He gets my goat."

He looked toward the willow tree. "Well, I delivered the boy safe and sound to his ma," he said. "I thank you for your horse and for your understanding."

"I never have seen a pluckier lad," the surgeon said. "He didn't even cry out when I set his leg. He just gritted his teeth and took it."

Jed went into the tent with the surgeon and took his rifle and slung it over his shoulder. The surgeon sat down behind the table.

"Captain," Jed said, "I got one more worry on my mind. The boy I share my tent with took sick about three days ago. He has a natural fear of doctors and hospitals and he wouldn't come to see you. He's a tall skinny boy, and he hasn't been eating since he took sick. I wonder if —"

The surgeon interrupted Jed. "I'll come over this evening and look in on him," he said. "In the meantime try to get him to eat something. He's just as well off in his tent as here. My tents are full, and I've been trying to get stoves for them since early in September."

"Thank you," Jed said. He told the surgeon how to find their tent, then he walked into camp and down the muddy company streets. After the woods and fields and the little farm, the camp seemed a place of unbroken ugliness. Men were sitting around telling stories or dozing in the sunlight. Some of them were playing cards, and here and there Jed saw someone cleaning his rifle.

When he got to the tent he lifted the flap to see if Jim was there, but the tent was empty. He guessed

73

that Jim had gone out for a little sunshine and fresh air. Sure enough he saw Jim standing nearby, watching a game of cards. Jed was suddenly struck by Jim's thinness. He didn't look lean and tall as Jed had always known him, but gaunt and sunken. He was pale as powder, and he was supporting himself by hanging onto a tent pole. When he caught sight of Jed his long face lit up in a smile. "Ready for that game of checkers?" he asked.

"Let's go over and fall in for some beans first," Jed said.

"I think I'll go back and lie down," Jim said. "I couldn't stand beans or salt pork either. About the only thing I could stomach is broth, and where would I get any broth?"

Jim moved toward their tent but halfway there he stopped and put his hand to his forehead and shook his head as if he felt dizzy.

Jed was worried. "I saw the surgeon and he told me to get some food into you," he said.

"I don't cotton much to doctors," Jim said.

"Any fool knows you got to eat," Jed said. "If broth is what you want I'll beg some for you if it takes me all afternoon."

"Doesn't this regiment drill any more?" Jim asked. "When we first got into this outfit the sound of the bugle pierced our ears from dawn to dusk."

"More than half of us are sick," said Jed, "and the camp has been such a mess of mud that everything has gone to pot. According to Charlie we're to shake ourselves out of the doldrums tomorrow. He says we might be moving soon. I guess they've decided this is no place for winter quarters."

"And right they are," said Jim.

They ducked into the tent. Jed fussed with Jim's blankets and Jim lay down and closed his eyes.

CHAPTER NINE

JED frowned and went out again and walked toward the mess tent. He knew it was a bad time to be begging for special food. At the mess tent, he saw a crowd of men waiting for Cookie to finish bustling and start serving. He knew they'd howl if he went to the back of the tent and held things up by talking to Cookie.

As Jed watched the men standing around with emptiness and sadness in their faces he felt a bitterness creeping into him. Most of them had joined the Army to fight for the Union. They had dreamed of going into battles with the banners flying and the bands playing. They had dreamed of a war that would move swiftly to its finish. Now they were sitting around in the mud without enough to eat, and their spirits were sinking lower every day. Abe Lincoln seemed a lot farther away from Jed now than he'd seemed when Will had talked about him back in Elkhorn.

Jed walked past the mess tent. Now that his temper had cooled he had it in mind to hunt for Davy and try to talk some sense into his head. Of course he couldn't come right out and tell him to keep away from the farm, but he might be able to figure some way of showing him that he wouldn't stand to gain by going there.

Jed found what he thought was Davy's company street. A supply train had just come in and some teamsters were unloading stores by a big supply dump at the end of a row of tents. A canvas roof was stretched over big poles to keep the stores dry, and a soldier was standing guard by one of the poles. The teamsters were rolling barrels out of the wagon and down a plank, laughing and singing and making a big noise.

Jed was just about to walk over to the guard and ask where he could find Davy when he caught sight of Davy walking along with two other soldiers. Without knowing why, Jed stepped behind a stack of boxes. Davy and his friends passed right near where he was standing. Davy was talking to the soldier on his left. The boy was short and even stockier than Davy. He had long black hair that stuck out from under his cap. The other soldier was tall and walked with a shuffle.

77

His arms hung loosely at his sides and he followed along after Davy like a stupid, faithful dog.

"We won't have no trouble finding the place," Davy was saying. "He went there on a horse and he came back the same way. He must have left a trail a mile wide. If we don't go right now, he and his friends will beat us to it."

One of the teamsters slammed a big box down beside Jed and the noise made Davy turn around. He looked straight at Jed. The others turned and stared too, but no one said a thing. Davy jerked his head and the three moved away, walking faster than before. Jed noticed that all of them carried rifles.

He stood and looked after the three soldiers as they swung around a tent and disappeared. He could see now that it was worse than useless to try to talk to Davy. If he picked a fight with him and his friends, everyone in the regiment would know about the farm by sundown. Jed found it easy to imagine what Captain Pike would say if he went to him and told him he wanted to protect a Rebel family.

Jed thought of Jim lying in the tent, weak and lonely and needing broth. Let those folks take care of themselves, he thought. Yanks are bound to pass that way sooner or later.

He found himself running to the mess tent.

I got to see Cookie, he thought.

Captain Pike was standing in front of the tent where the boys were eating. If he caught Jed inside the mess tent, especially at mealtime, he wouldn't like it much. Jed slipped into the tent and stood in the back waiting for a chance to talk to Cookie. Through the front flap he saw Captain Pike moving away, and he breathed a little easier. Finally he caught Cookie's eye. "I need to talk to you, Cookie," he said.

"Tarnation, boy, I'm busy," Cookie said. "Go around front and get some pork and beans and I'll talk to you later."

Jed's voice went up a notch. "Cookie, listen to me a minute. I'm not looking for a handout."

"Just a minute," he said.

As Cookie walked away Jed tightened his hands into fists. He couldn't help thinking of that pretty woman with her fool musket and that little boy and his sister and the dog that looked like Brownie. It almost drove

79

him crazy to think of Davy and his friends wrecking their place and taking their food. He looked over at Cookie, who was talking to one of his helpers. Finally Cookie handed the man a big ladle and walked back to Jed. "What is it, boy?" he asked. "I got no time to talk to you now."

"I know," Jed said. "Well, my partner Jim is sick and he needs broth. The surgeon said to get food into him. He can't take solid food now and —"

Cookie smiled a jolly smile and snapped his fingers in front of Jed's face. "You go out front," he said, "and get some beans for yourself, and I'll fix up some soup for Jim in about half an hour."

"But," Jed said, "there's more to it than that. The rest of it you have to take partly on faith. . . . "

"I like you, boy," Cookie said, "but you'll get me mad in a minute. You just do as I say."

Jed was near panic now. "Cookie," he said, "I'm in a terrible fix. For the love of mercy believe me and do me a favor. As soon as you can get away, take some soup to Jim and nurse him a little. I can't do it myself. I've got something else I have to do right now."

Cookie looked hard at Jed for what seemed a full minute. "You can trust me to take care of your partner, boy," he said, "but don't be gettin' yourself into any trouble."

80

CHAPTER TEN

JED pushed past the boys out front and along the company street and out past the wagons and horses and past the hospital tents. He thought fleetingly of asking the surgeon for his horse, but Jed knew the surgeon would probably say no and do his best to keep Jed from going. He ran out across the field and tried to slice between the pickets, but he was hailed by the man standing guard by the willow. Jed just waved and kept on running. He thought of yelling back that he was off for some hunting, but then he realized that he'd left his rifle in the tent with Jim.

That brought him up short. He still had his bayonet, but he knew he'd never use that. He stood for a minute looking back. The picket hailed him again and that settled it. Jed wheeled around and bolted into a thicket that was nearly a foot under water. Sometimes

81

the water came to his knees but he kept plowing along until the ground rose a little. Everything seemed different from this morning. He couldn't have picked a worse place to start out. Now his boots were filled with water and his trousers were soaked, and he already felt winded. For a while he wondered if he was going in the right direction, but at last he reached the stream at a place where the banks were low and irregular. This morning, when he was high and dry on the back of a horse and not in a hurry, the trip through the lowland was bothersome, but now it was like a nightmare. It took an eternity to skirt the curves and pools and climb over the tangle of vines. He cursed himself. No one but a fool would go through a swamp with no rifle or pistol to fight off three boys who were armed. All he had to do was turn and go back. But he knew if he did he would never forgive himself.

His boots squelched and his feet were cold but he felt more hopeful as he came to drier land. He ran along a corridor of slippery leaves until he felt a sharp pain in his lungs. His foot caught against a root and he pitched forward to the ground. He lay motionless with his fingers digging into the cold, wet leaves and then he raised his head. His eye caught something moving off to the right. He was about to get to his feet when he saw a big ugly cottonmouth slithering along just ahead of him. Jed lay still, holding his breath, ready to jump up if he had to. The snake paused not ten feet in front of him and raised its head as if uncertain which way to go. Then it moved off toward the river. Jed watched in fascinated horror as it slid along, making the leaves stir ever so slightly as it passed. The consarned thing must have been at least four feet long.

He stood up slowly and let out his breath in a quiet rush. He hadn't been wrong when he'd told Davy this was snake country. Why the devil couldn't that snake have frightened Davy out of his wits instead of him?

Jed stood and strained his ears for sounds of Davy and his friends, but he couldn't hear a thing and he started walking again. Thoughts of that snake made him keep his eyes on the ground, but whenever the underbrush thinned a little he looked ahead and listened.

As he worked his way through the woods he could see signs.

There were hoofprints and broken branches and trampled grasses made by the surgeon's horse. Once in a while he saw footprints and he knew that Davy and his friends were somewhere ahead of him.

Jed came to a sudden stop when he recognized the shallow place in the stream where he had watered the horse and they had crossed the stream. He knelt down and scooped up some clear, cold water and dashed it into his face.

The water refreshed him and he waded across the stream and dug into the far bank and moved onto the higher, wooded ground. Now he felt stronger and he began to run. He moved as quietly as possible but once in a while a branch cracked under his foot and he worried that he might round a stand of trees to be faced suddenly by Davy and his friends.

Jed's imagination began to play tricks on him and he thought he saw the woman standing on the hill, shooting her musket over Davy's head, and Davy raising his rifle to shoot and the woman crumpling to the ground. In his vision he saw the boy limping out of the house and getting hit with the butt of one of the rifles and the girl watching from the door and screaming and screaming.

His vision made Jed run faster, and other pictures flashed across his mind. It seemed too late to save the people at the farm, and now he saw the house on fire and the barn and the great, gray horses rearing and bellowing and crashing through the side of the flaming, blackened shed.

Jed's eyes clouded and his feet stumbled. As he came out into a clear place of rocks and grass, it seemed that he was barely moving at all. He felt suddenly sick and fell forward in the grass and lay still. He felt that he had come to the end of his strength, that it was useless to try to go on. Except for his hearing, his senses seemed dead.

He lay there for what seemed a long time, aware only of the gentle, dry sounds of the grass. Finally he opened his eyes and raised himself up. He stood, a little unsteady at first, and looked down at his feet and moved his toes in the wet insides of his boots. Then he remembered why he was here and he began to move along the stream again. He walked now, knowing that there was a limit to his endurance and that he needed strength for what was ahead.

Jed went through the last patch of woods with great care. The farm was just ahead and he must think of what he would do. He knew that his only chance lay in surprise. Talking to Davy was worse than useless. Thoughts of Davy made him boiling mad.

Just ahead, Jed saw that the trees were thinning and beyond them was the tawny grass of the field. He looked to the ridge and his eyes fastened on three figures that were etched against the sky. He moved fast, cutting through the grass as quiet as any Indian. When he was near enough he could see that Davy was between the other soldiers. They moved down the slope holding their rifles ready. As they rounded the trees Jed could barely wait to close in on them.

He was fired with strength and impatience, but he moved up slowly until he saw the figure of the girl in the door. Her hand went up to her mouth and she stifled a scream.

Then Davy stopped cold and Jed came up and jumped him and knocked his rifle out of his hands. Davy's jaw dropped and his eyes bugged out and Jed swung and smashed his fist right into the middle of Davy's face. Blood spurted out of his nose and ran down all over his face, but he came toward Jed, swinging wildly. Jed ducked and they both hit the ground in a tangle. Jed found Davy's knee pressing into his chest and he saw Davy's face hanging over him, twisted by an ugly grin. Just when it seemed he might lose his wind, Jed gave a lurch and Davy lost his balance and rolled off to the side. Jed was on him like a flash and sent a lightning punch into Davy's stomach. Then Davy came up again, staggering a little, and Jed landed a punch on the side of his jaw that cracked the air and sent him spinning.

As Jed came around he caught a glimpse of Davy's rifle lying on the ground. He took it in his hands and brought his head up and things began to come into focus. The short, stocky boy was coming toward him with the butt of his rifle raised. The tall boy was standing stupidly with his bayonet fixed, looking at Davy as if he couldn't understand this fight between Yankee

soldiers. Jed brought Davy's rifle up and the sight of
it stopped the short boy in his tracks.

Jed looked at him with a face like stone. "Drop
the rifle," he said in a steady rasping voice.

Now something was happening that the tall boy
could understand. He was about to raise his rifle when

Jed turned and covered him. "Now git," he said, his eye on the other two boys. "You can go back proud that you tried to raid a little farm where there's only a woman and her children."

The tall boy turned like a funny old camel and walked off down the hill. His tameness made Jed want to laugh. Davy was sitting up and shaking his head. The shorter boy looked from Jed to Davy and back again. "What's your stake in this farm?" he asked.

"No stake," Jed said. "A little boy from here wandered near camp this morning and broke his leg. When he was fit for travel I brought him back. I liked the boy and I liked his ma and I knew they had barely enough food for the winter so I didn't want to see their place raided."

"Sure you didn't just want the pickin's for yourself?"

"I've eaten nothing here," Jed said, "nor will I, and I don't plan on coming back here either."

"That's good enough for me," the short, stocky boy said. "If I take up my rifle you can trust me to move along."

"Go ahead," said Jed.

The boy reached to the ground for his rifle while Jed covered him, and he turned and followed the tall boy past the trees and over the hill.

Davy looked groggy but he raised himself up to

one knee, and his bloody lips began to move. "I see you got reinforcements," he said bitterly.

Jed turned and saw the woman standing quietly, watching, with her musket held loosely in her hands. The little dog was yelping around her and he came toward the soldiers. Then he turned in a fright and ran back again. The boy was standing behind her on one leg, watching Jed with a big smile on his face.

Jed turned back to Davy. He pointed Davy's rifle at the ground and fired it off. The short, stocky boy had just reached the top of the rise and he broke and ran when he heard the shot.

Jed took the bayonet off the rifle and stuck it into his belt. Davy's defiance hadn't quite boiled away. "I'll see you get the devil when we get back to camp," he said. "They could string you up for this."

Jed held the rifle toward Davy. "They'd string you up right beside me," he said. He gave Davy a long look. "Your kind is a bully in camp and a shirker in battle."

Davy's face told Jed that his words had hit Davy where he hurt the most.

"Now hand over your cartridge box," Jed said, "and you can have your rifle back."

Davy did as he was told and took his rifle.

"I'll see you get your bayonet and cartridge box back," Jed said.

He watched Davy get up and stumble down the hill. The dog was still yelping and now he got bolder and ran to Jed, wagging his tail and jumping up. Jed kneeled down and patted him and the dog was quiet and licked his hand. The boy hopped after the dog. "You look a terrible fright," he said. "I hope they give you a new uniform."

"New uniforms are as scarce as hen's teeth," Jed said picking up his cap from where it had fallen, "but I'm handy with a needle and thread."

Jed looked toward the house and saw the old musket leaning against the wall beside the door. "Where's your ma now?" he asked. "She was here just a minute ago."

"She'll be back," the boy said, "but my sister's been told to stay indoors."

The woman came out of the house with something in her hand and walked up to them. "I'd like for you to have this," she said.

Jed looked at the shining thing and took it and held it. "Why, ma'am," he said.

"It's a brass candleholder," the woman said. "Philip's pa carries one like it. Just unscrew the cover. The holder and candle are inside."

Jed unscrewed the cover and screwed in the holder and set the candle in its place. He grinned and then

90

he took it all apart again and closed it and put it into his breast pocket.

"Thank you, ma'am," he said. He bent down to pat the dog again and then he said, "I wish I could stay awhile but I want to get back to my sick partner."

He shook the boy's hand. "Good-by, Philip," he said.

Jed smiled at the woman and turned and walked past the trees and the barn, through the tall tawny grass and over the hill.

Before he went into the woods he stopped for a minute and looked up the hill. He heard the sound of a voice and then the boy came to the crest of the hill. He waved wildly and the little dog jumped around him, lively as ever.

Jed raised his arm high and waved and then, as suddenly as they had come, the boy and the dog disappeared. Jed looked for a minute at the place where they had been and then his eyes traveled along the blue arch of the sky until he was looking straight overhead where a mass of white clouds moved with the breeze. He saw a lone bird far above him, silhouetted against the clouds and drifting and flying toward the west.

He watched the bird until it disappeared from sight and then he slapped his breast pocket and settled his cap on his head and walked into the woods. It was getting chilly again. The shadows were longer and the woods were darker but now Jed knew his way. He was filled with a strange happiness.

For the first time in weeks his thoughts turned to the fights that he knew must lie ahead. It seemed that he was more afraid of battle now than before the fight at Shiloh but he loved his country and he believed that the Union must be saved. He knew that when the time came he would measure up.

CHAPTER ELEVEN

JED found his way through the lowland again and when he could see the top of the willow tree he yelled to the picket. As he passed the man the picket took one look at his uniform and stared at him as if he was crazy, but he let Jed pass without a fuss.

Jed went straight into camp and walked fast through the rows of tents until he came to his own.

Jim was awake. "Where you been, Jed?" he asked. "Cookie said you were all worked up about something."

Jed put on his coat and stretched out on his blankets. "I'll tell you the story tomorrow," he said. "Right now I'm tuckered out."

He propped up on one elbow and turned to Jim. "Did Cookie take care of you?" he asked.

"He sure did," said Jim. "He brooded around here like an old hen and he tried to ladle soup into my mouth until I showed him I could do it myself. He left a big chunk of salt pork."

Jim took the pork out of one of his coat pockets and handed it to Jed. "Eat it all," he said. "I have no stomach for the stuff."

Jed munched away at the pork. "Good old Cookie," he said.

He looked over and saw that Jim was dozing again.

Jed dozed off too and when he woke it was dusk. He stirred and rolled over. He heard Jim's voice in the dark. "You and that fat old mess sergeant are as good as any mother," he said.

Jed chuckled. "Let's have that game of checkers now."

"Can't see your hand in front of your face much less a checkerboard," Jim said, "and we got no candles left."

Jed reached into his breast pocket and took out something round and shining. He unscrewed the cover and screwed in the holder and set the candle in its place and fumbled for a match and lit the candle.

Jim grinned as the light of the candle caught the brass and made it shine like gold. "Where'd you get that, old partner?" he asked.

Jed smiled and moved the first checker. "Maybe you'd like to hear that story now," he said.

The role of author is a fairly new one for Peter Burchard, but as an illustrator he has more than fifty books for both adults and children to his credit. Mr. Burchard's latest book as author for Coward-McCann is NORTH BY NIGHT, the story of capture and escape from a Southern prison camp during the Civil War.

Peter says that though he gets a big kick out of non-fiction writing, "it isn't as much fun as writing a story like JED. You've got to reach deeper to write something like JED and it's just that much more rewarding."

Peter Burchard lives in New City, New York, with his wife, Betsey, and three children, Lee, Peter Jr. and Laura.